About the Author

MICHAEL P. SPRADLIN is the author of the *New York Times* bestseller *It's Beginning to Look a Lot Like Zombies!* as well as several children's picture books, the novels and manga volumes in the Spy Goddess series, and the Youngest Templar novels. He lives in Michigan with his family.

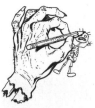

About the Illustrator

JEFF WEIGEL is the illustrator of the *New York Times* bestseller *It's Beginning to Look a Lot Like Zombies!* and he wrote, illustrated, and designed the children's picture books *Atomic Ace (He's Just My Dad)*, *Atomic Ace and the Robot Rampage*, and the historical graphic adventure novel *Thunder from the Sea*. He also created the character of the Sphinx for Image Comics' Big Bang series, for which he both writes and illustrates.

Every
ZOMBIE
Eats Sombody Sometime

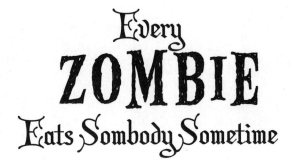

Also by Michael P. Spradlin and Jeff Weigel

It's Beginning to Look a Lot Like Zombies!: A Book of Zombie Christmas Carols

Also by Michael P. Spradlin

SPY GODDESS NOVELS

Live and Let Shop

To Hawaii, with Love

SPY GODDESS MANGA

The Chase for the Chalice

The Quest for the Lance

THE YOUNGEST TEMPLAR NOVELS

Keeper of the Grail

Trail of Fate

PICTURE BOOKS

The Legend of Blue Jacket

Texas Rangers: Legendary Lawmen

Daniel Boone's Great Escape

Off Like the Wind!: The First Ride of the Pony Express

Baseball from A to Z

Every
ZOMBIE
Eats Sombody Sometime

A BOOK OF ZOMBIE LOVE SONGS

Michael P. Spradlin
Illustrations by Jeff Weigel

HARPER

NEW YORK • LONDON • TORONTO • SYDNEY

HARPER

HarperCollins books may be purchased for educational, business, or sales promotional use. For information please write: Special Markets Department, HarperCollins Publishers, 10 East 53rd Street, New York, NY 10022.

FIRST EDITION

Illustrations by Jeff Weigel
Designed by Justin Dodd

Library of Congress Cataloging-in-Publication Data is available upon request.

ISBN 978-0-06-201182-4

10 11 12 13 14   OV/RRD   10 9 8 7 6 5 4 3 2 1

For Kelly. As Always.

CONTENTS

ZOMBIES NEED LOVE (SONGS) TOO

Whither the poor Zombie? The Undead. The Revenant. The non-stationary cadaver as it were. When our attention is focused on hacking and whacking and we stand knee deep in arterial spray, do we ever stop and consider the thoughts and needs of the beings we're so happily dispatching? Do we realize these poor, eternally damned creatures were once our friends, our neighbors, and yes . . .

Even our lovers.

What this book seeks to do is restore a little of the balance to a world gone haywire in the coming Zombie Apocalypse. When you're forced to put down your wife or husband, boyfriend or girlfriend, partner or POSSLQ (Person of the Opposite Sex Sharing Living Quarters), perhaps you'll want to remember some of the good times. When your love was new, and you could sit together on the porch swing, sharing a tall, cold glass of lemonade, without worrying your loved one would turn into a vicious, soulless, brain-eating Zombie.

Zombies seldom get a fair shake. You see, most of the time, as the Undead flock around us, we're desperately fighting for our lives. When you're busy killing ghouls, you don't have time to think about things like love, and that's too bad. And it's the reason I wrote this book.

Perhaps you had a favorite love song you sang to each other. Now, when you are forced to kill the one you're with, you can share one last memory of "your" song before you send that slobbering, drooling, gray-matter-munching, shuffling pile of human tissue straight to hell. Think of it as the greatest collection of love songs for the Zombie age. Maybe the two of you had a thing for the Beatles, or Elvis. Perhaps Motown or Sinatra was your musical muse. No matter what you might have enjoyed sharing, this book offers you a wide selection of hits to choose from.

And for those of you still doubting the coming Apocalypse, let me assure you, it will happen. In fact, during my research for this book, I was shocked to discover Zombies have a long and storied tradition of creating music.

How else do you explain Keith Richards?

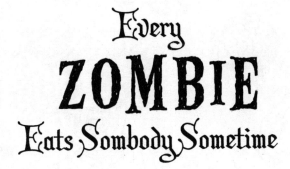

Every
ZOMBIE
Eats Sombody Sometime

My Fear of a Clown

Sung to the tune of "Tears of a Clown"
by Smokey Robinson and the Miracles

Oh yeah, yeah, yeah,

Now if there's some blood on my face,
It's only there when I bite the public,
But when it comes down to chewing you,
Now honey, that's quite a Zombie subject.
But don't let my blank expression
Give you the undead impressions.
Really I'm dead, oh I'm deader than dead.
You're gone and I'm hurtin' so bad.
The dead can't pretend to be glad.

Chorus
Now there's some bad things known to man,
But ain't too much badder than
A real Zombie clown, when he's chowin' down.
Uh hum, oh yeah baby.

Now if I appear to be undead,
It's only to camouflage my sickness.
And honey to hide my slime I try
To cover this virus with a show of madness.

But don't let my fate convince you
That I've been undead since you
Decided to go. Oh, I'll eat you so.
I'm bit and I want you to know,
But for others I shuffle so slow, ooh yeah.

Repeat Chorus

Just like Romero did,
I try to keep the undead hid.
Lurching in the public eye
But in my lonely room I died.
I'm a Zombie clown,
And I'm chowin' down, oh yeah, baby baby.
Now if there's some brains in this place,
Don't let my blank expression
Give you the undead impressions.
Don't let my smile at your fear
Make you think that I can't share.
When really I'm dead
Oh I'm really dead . . .

You'll Scream in Fear

Sung to the tune of "Tracks of My Tears"
by Smokey Robinson and the Miracles

People say there's no life at our party,
Because I ate a brain or two.
Although I might be munching loud and hearty,
Deep inside I'm goo.
Don't take a good look at my face,
You'll see my nose looks out of place.
If you come closer, I'll chew off your face.
You'll scream in fear.
I eat you, eat you.
Since you ran from me if you see me chowin' down
On some random girl.
Although she may taste great,
Darlin' don't hesitate,
Because I'm comin' after you too.
Don't take a good look at my face,
You'll see my nose it looks out of place.
If you look closer, you'll see my disgrace.
You'll scream in fear.
I'll eat you, eat you.
Don't take a good look at my face,
You'll see my nose looks out of place.

If you come closer, I'll rip off your face.
You'll scream in fear.
I eat you, eat you.

Outside . . . I'm masticating,
Inside . . . reanimating.
A Zombie clown, oh yeah,
Since you put me down.
Your brain is my makeup,
I wear since I tried to eat you.
Don't take a good look at my face,
You'll see my nose looks out of place.
If you come closer, I'll bite off your face.
You'll scream in fear.

Every Zombie Eats Somebody Sometime

Sung to the tune of "Everybody Loves Somebody Sometime"
by Dean Martin

Every Zombie eats somebody sometime,
Everybody turns Zombie somehow.
Something in your bite just told me,
My turning is now.

Every Zombie chews somebody someplace,
There's no telling where they may appear.
Something in the air keeps spreadin',
The virus is here.

If I had enough sharp weapons
I'd hack away at the Zombie swarms.
Then every single undead hour,
Every Zombie would be looking for his arms.

Every Zombie eats somebody sometime,
And though the virus was overdue,
Your brains made it well worth waiting,
For munching on you.

If I had enough sharp weapons
I'd hack away at the Zombie swarms.

Then every single undead hour,
Every Zombie would be looking for his arms.

Every Zombie eats somebody sometime,
And though the virus was overdue,
Your brains made it well worth waiting,
For munching on you.

Soda Shoppe

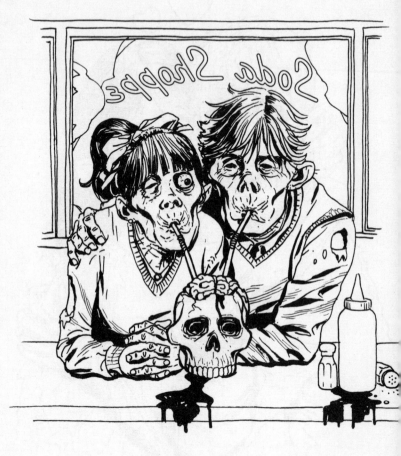

You've Lost That Livin' Feeling

Sung to the tune of "You've Lost That Lovin' Feeling" by the Righteous Brothers

You never chew on eyes anymore when the virus trips.
And your skin's tenderest while it peels off in my fingertips.
You're trying hard not to vomit (baby).
But baby, baby, you're rotting . . .

You've lost that livin' feeling,
Whoa, that livin' feeling,
You've lost that livin' feeling,
Now it's gone . . . gone . . . moan . . . woooooah.

Now there's an undead look in my eyes
when I reach for you.
And now you're starting to criticize all the things I chew.
It makes me just keep on trying (baby).
'Cause baby, like me you are dying.

You lost that livin' feeling,
Whoa, that livin' feeling,
You've lost that livin' feeling,
Now it's gone . . . gone . . . moan . . . woooooah.

Baby, baby, I chow down on some knees for you.

If you would only bite me like I just bit you, yeah.

We found a brain . . . a brain . . . a brain you don't find every day.

So don't . . . don't . . . don't . . . don't you run away.

Baby (baby), baby (baby),
I beg of you please . . . please,
I need a brain (I need a brain),
I need a brain (I need a brain),
For a tasty snack (for a tasty snack),
For a tasty snack (for a tasty snack).

Virus took that livin' feeling,
Whoa, that livin' feeling,
We lost that livin' feeling,
'Cause it's gone . . . gone . . . moan,
and I can't go on,
noooo . . .

Bring back that livin' feeling,
Whoa, that livin' feeling,
Bring back that livin' feeling,
'Cause it's gone . . . gone

Can You Find My Thumb Tonight?

Sung to the tune of "Can You Feel the Love Tonight" by Elton John

Why didn't we surrender, we should have run away,
When the tide of a zombie horde wasn't turned away.
An apocalyptic moment, we're infected through and through,
It's enough for this walking cadaver to try and eat you too.

And can you find my thumb tonight?
It was here somewhere!
I've been bit by this undead zombie,
Now my thumb's in your hair!

And can you find my thumb tonight?
It's a survival test.
This virus will turn kings and vagabonds,
Along with all the rest.

There's a time for everyone if they only learn
That the zombie apocalypse infects us and we turn.
There's a rhyme and reason to the hordes outside,
When the heart of this just-turned revenant is swallowed
Down with yours.

And can you find my thumb tonight?
It was here somewhere!

It's enough for this infected wanderer,
Oh look, it's in your hair.
And can you find my thumb tonight,
Wait! It's in my chest.
We will feed on kings and vagabonds
And eat all of the rest.

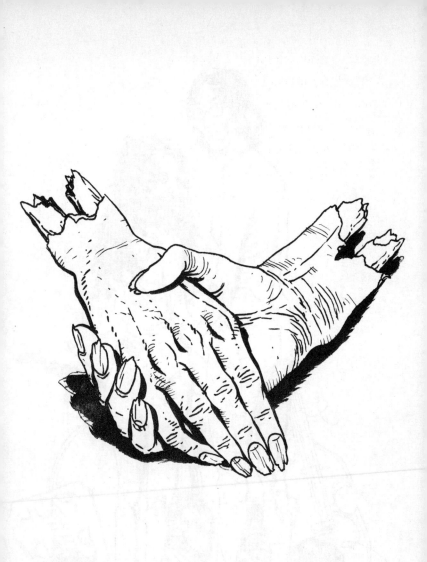

PAUL IS DEAD!

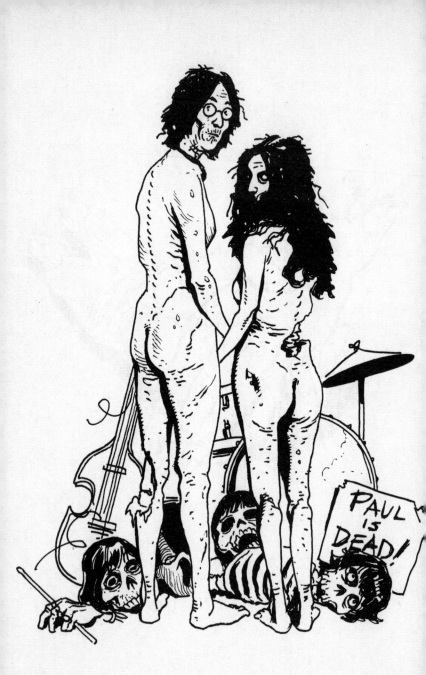

Imagine (There's No Zombies)

Sung to the tune of "Imagine" by John Lennon

Imagine there's no Zombies,
It's easy, just don't die.
No hell around us,
Somehow we'd get by.
Imagine all the undead
Dying off today.

Imagine there's no virus,
No undead to chew.
Nothing to kill or chase us,
And no Apocalypse too.
Imagine all the Zombies
Dying at our feet.

You may say that I'm a screamer,
But there're many more than one.
I hope you are not turned
And live free of Zombie scum.

Imagine no more weapons,
Just try it and you can.
No need for hand grenades nor axes,
A surviving world of man.

Imagine all the Zombies
Dying at your feet.

You may say that I'm a screamer,
But there're many more than one.
I hope someday you'll join us
In a world with no Zombie Scum.

T 2553
Capitol
YESTERDAY · DR. ROBERT
I'M ONLY SLEEPING · AND YOUR BIRD CAN SING
WE CAN WORK IT OUT · DAY TRIPPER
NOWHERE MAN · WHAT GOES ON?
DRIVE MY CAR · IF I NEEDED SOMEONE
ACT NATURALLY
The Beatles
Yesterday
And Today

BRAINS TODAY

Sung to the tune of "Yesterday" by the Beatles

Yesterday,
All the Zombies seemed so far away,
Now it looks as though they're here to stay,
Oh, I'm hungry for something gray.

Suddenly,
I'm just half the man I used to be,
Parts are falling off of me,
Oh the virus came on suddenly.

Why she
Had to bite me I don't know, she wouldn't say.
I said,
Something's wrong, now I want some brains.

Yesterday,
My hunger did not drive me on this way,
Now I need to munch on something gray,
Oh, I was human yesterday.

Why she
Had to bite me I don't know, she wouldn't say.
I said,

Something's wrong, now I long for something gray.

Yesterday,

My need for brains is here to stay,

Now I will munch on something gray,

Oh, I believe in brains today.

Mm-mm-mm-mm-mm-mm-mm. (bbbbbrrrrraaaaiiiiiiiinnnnnsssss)

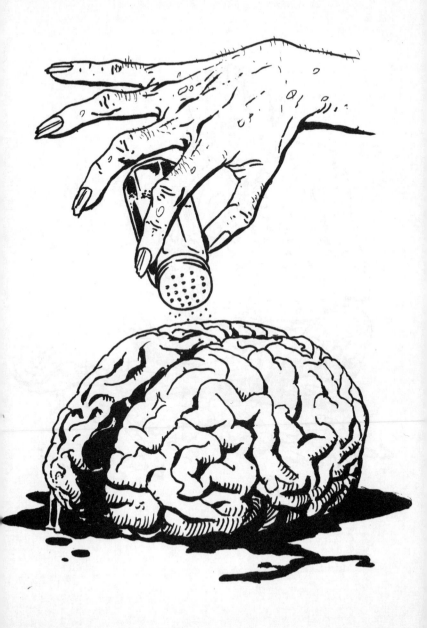

LOVES ME
LOVES ME NOT

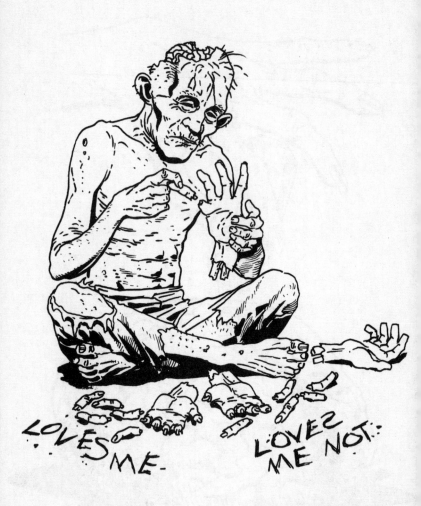

I Want to Eat Your Hand

Sung to the tune of "I Want to Hold Your Hand" by the Beatles

Oh yeah, I've turned into something,
You just won't understand.
When I say that you're delicious
I want to eat your hand,
I want to eat your hand,
I want to eat your hand.

Oh please, say I'm a Zombie,
I'm eating your brain pan,
And please, don't slay me
You'll let me eat your hand.
Now let me eat your hand,
I want to eat your hand.

And when I eat brains I feel happy inside.
It's such a feeling that my gore
You can't hide, you can't hide, you can't hide.

Yeah, you've got that large brain,
I think you won't understand.
When I'll say I'm so hungry
I want to eat your hand,

I want to eat your hand,
I want to eat your hand.

And when I eat brains I feel happy inside.
It's such a feeling that my love
You can't hide, you can't hide, you can't hide.

Yeah, you've got that big brain,
You just won't understand.
When I'll say I'm so hungry
And munchin' on your hand,
I want to nosh your hand,
I want to chew your hand.

That'll Be the Day (When I Make You Die)

Sung to the tune of "That'll Be the Day" by Buddy Holly and the Crickets

Well, that'll be the day, when you say goodbye,
Yes, that'll be the day, when I make you die,
You say you're gonna eat me, you know you can try,
'Cause that'll be the day when you die.

Well, you went after me, hungry for brains,
All your bites and noshing you left me in pain.
Well, you know there's my machete,
Unless you run, my baby,
That someday, I'll kill you.

Well, that'll be the day, when you say goodbye,
Yes, that'll be the day, when I make you die,
You say you're gonna eat me, you know can try,
'Cause I'll put a bullet right in your eye.

Well, that'll be the day, when you say goodbye,
Yes, that'll be the day, when I make you die,
You say you're gonna eat me, you know you can try,
'Cause that'll be the day when you die.

Well, when that Zombie did his part,

He bit you, the virus did start.
So we had to part, and I will kill you,
You come after me and you say it coldly
That someday, you're gonna chew.

Well, that'll be the day, when you say goodbye,
Yes, that'll be the day, when I make you die,
You say you're gonna eat me, you know you can try,
'Cause that'll be the day when you die.

Well, that'll be the day, chew-chew,
I'll make you die, chew-chew,
Your face will decay, chew-chew,
You I will slay.

DEAR JOHN

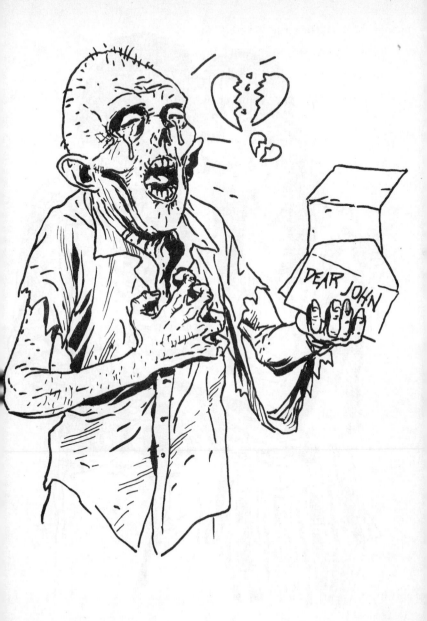

I Bit You Babe

Sung to the tune of "I Got You Babe" by Sonny and Cher

Her: They say we're dead and we don't know
We won't find out until we show.
Him: Well, I don't know why you're so blue
'Cause you bit me, and baby I bit you.

Him: Babe,
Both: I bit you babe,
I bit you babe.

Her: They say eatin' brains won't pay the rent,
Before we're burned, our hungers all been spent.
Him: I guess that's so, we don't eat a lot,
But at least I'm sure of all the brains we got.

Him: Babe,
Both: I bit you babe,
I bit you babe.

Him: I got turned in the spring
I bit off your wedding ring.
Her: And when I'm sad, you eat a clown,
And if I get scared, you're always chowin' down

Her: Don't let them say eatin' brains is wrong
'Cause I don't care, they make us strong.
Him: Your little hand came off in mine,
There ain't no cowering victim we can't find.

Him: Babe,
Both: I bit you babe,
I bit you babe.

Him: I got you to eat my hand.
Her: I bit you undead again.
Him: I bit you to walk with me.
Her: I bit you now stalk with me,
I bit you to kiss goodnight,
I bit you it feels so right,
I bit you, I won't let go,
I got you to love brains so.

Both: I bit you babe,
I bit you babe,
I bit you babe,
I bit you babe,
I bit you babe.

You Are So Edible

Sung to the tune of "You Are So Beautiful" by Joe Cocker

You are so edible,
You see.
You are so edible,
You flee.
Don't you scream,
Your brain is what I hoped for,
Your brain is what I need.
You are so edible,
You see.

You are so delicious,
Says me.
You are so delicious,
Let's see.
Don't you scream,
You're as tasty as I hoped for,
As tasty as I need.
You are so delicious,
You see.

You are so chewable,
Don't flee.

You are so chewable,
For me.
Don't you scream,
You're everything I turned for,
You undead is what I need.
You are so edible,
Don't flee.

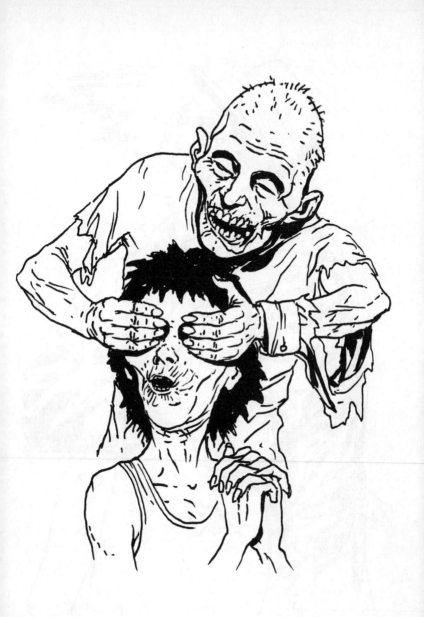

Zombies in the Night

Sung to the tune of "Strangers in the Night" by Frank Sinatra

Zombies in the night, consuming organs
Shuffling through the night, what were the chances
They would eat our brains, before the night was through?

Something in their bite was so inviting.
Chewing on a brain was so exciting
Something in my heart, told me I must bite you!

Strangers in the night,
Two lonely monsters. Zombies in the night,
Up to the moment, we ate brain Jell-O™, little did we know
Reanimation's just a bite away, warm blood tastes great this way.

And. . .

Ever since that night we've been undeader,
Revenant at first sight, chomping forever.
It turned out so right, two Zombies in the night.

Dowedowechewdududud.
Munchymunchymunch.
Snacksnackysnacksnack.

My Heart Will Taste Good

Sung to the tune of "My Heart Will Go On" by Céline Dion

Every night in my screams
I see you. I fear you.
That is how I know you are gone.

Even at this distance
And undead between us,
You have come to turn and live on.

Near, far, how undead you are,
I believe you my heart does taste good.
Once more you smash through the door
And you're here in my room
And my heart will taste fresh and good.

You can bite me one time,
It shortens a lifetime,
And never be full till we're one.

Love was when I stabbed you,
One true time I had to,
In my life I know Zombies go on.

Near, far, how undead you are,
I believe you the heart does taste good.
Once more you kick down the door
And you're here in my house
And my brains will live on and on.

There is some love that will not
go away.

You're here, now I'm full of fear,
And I know that my heart will taste good.
You'll slay forever this way,
I am dead on my floor
And my heart will taste fresh and good.

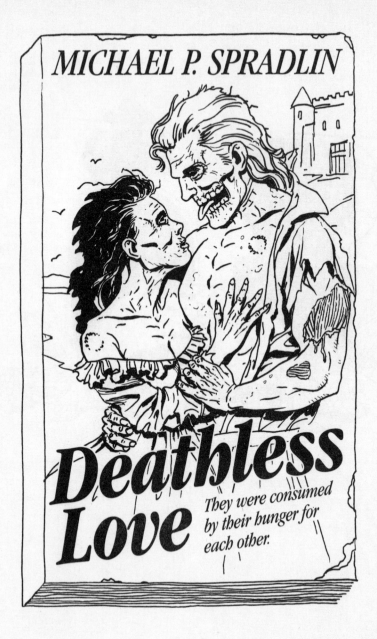

MICHAEL P. SPRADLIN

Deathless Love

They were consumed by their hunger for each other.

My Undead Love

Sung to the tune of "Endless Love" by Lionel Richie and Diana Ross

Dead love,
You're only food in my life,
In this damn zombie blight.

My first turn,
You're every bite that I take,
Each shuffling step I make.

And I
(I-I-I-I-I)
I want to chew
All the brains with you,
No other dead will do . . .

Eat your eyes,
Your eyes, your eyes,
They are no longer there,
Ooh yes, you will truly be
My undead love.

Two hearts,
Two hearts, so let's eat one.
Our lives were just undone.

Forever
(Ohhhhhh)
I'll probably chew your arms,
I can't resist your arms.

And love,
Oh, love
I'll always drool
For you,
I'm sure
You know I've no mind.
Oh, you know I've no mind.

'Cause you,
You're just a meal to me.
Oh
I know
I know
I've found in you
My undead love.

Oooh-woow.
Boom, boom.
Boom, boom, boom, boom, boom.
Boom, boom, boom, boom, boom.

Oooh, and love,
Oh, love
I'll always drool
For you,
I'm sure
You know I've no mind.
Oh you know—
I've no mind.

And, YES,
You'll be the only one
'Cause I can't be denied
This hunger inside
And I'll fill it all with you
My love
My love, my love,
My undead love.

Fifty Ways to Eat Your Lover

Sung to the tune of "Fifty Ways to Leave Your Lover" by Paul Simon

"The problem is all because you're dead,"
She informed me.
Brain love is easy when you
Become a zombie.
I'd like to kill you as you struggle
To eat me.
There's at least fifty ways
To eat your lover.

She said it's really not my desire
To steal food.
Furthermore, I hope my feeding
Won't be considered rude,
But I'll treat myself
At the risk of being crude.
There must be fifty ways
To eat your lover.
Fifty ways to eat your lover.

You just tear off his back, Jack.
Chomp on a hand, Stan.
You don't need to be coy, Roy.

Just get yourself free,
Pull out his guts, Gus.
You don't need to digest much,
Just bite off a knee, Lee,
And be a Zombie.

She said it bothers me too
To see you not eat brains.
I wish there were some here I could catch
To make you eat again.
I said I'll decapitate that
And would you please be plain
About the fifty ways.

She said the Zombies will
Just chew on it tonight
And I'm certain in the morning
You'll see the zombie blight.
And then she bit me
And I knew that she probably was right.
There's at least fifty ways
To eat your lover.
Fifty ways to chew your lover.

Eat Caroline

Sung to the tune of "Sweet Caroline" by Neil Diamond

When it began,
I see the Virus showin',
But then I know it's growin' strong.
Turned in the spring
And more turned in the summer,
Who'd have believed you'd become undead.

Hands, clutchin' hands,
Screamin' now,
Bitin' me,
Bitin' you.

Eat Caroline,
Intestines never seemed so good.
I'm now undead,
Can't believe they are so good.

But now I walk through the night,
And I don't seem so hungry,
We fill it up with lots of goo.
And though I hurt,
Someone ripped off my shoulder,
It doesn't hurt when I bite you.

Warm, blood is warm,
Screamin' out,
Bitin' me,
Bitin' you.
Eat Caroline,
Intestines never seemed so good.
I'm now undead,
Can't believe they are so good.

It's go, go, go.

Eat Caroline,
Intestines never seemed so good.
I'm now undead,
Can't believe they are so good.
Eat Caroline.

TYPE
A

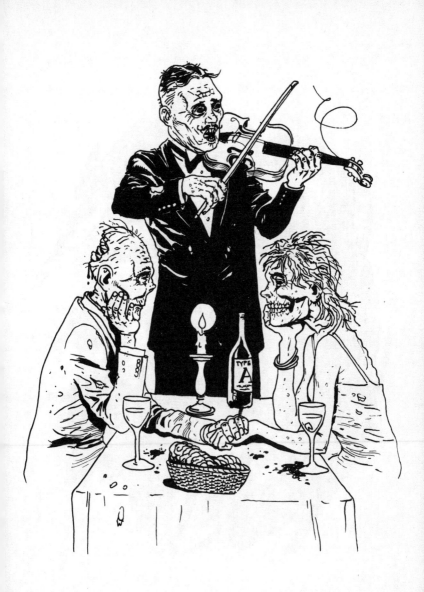

I Can't Stop Chewing You

Sung to the tune of "I Can't Stop Loving You" by Ray Charles

(I can't stop chewing you)
They ate up my brain.
I live in memory of the living times.
(I can't stop eating you)
It's useless to slay,
So I'll just live my life in screams of yesterday.
(Screams of yesterday)
Those fresh brains that we once chewed,
Tho' long ago, they still make me drool.
They say it's time to eat a broken heart,
But time stands still when the virus starts.

(I can't stop chewing you)
I'll eat up your mind.
To live in memories of those undead times.
(I can't stop chasing you)
It's useless to slay,
So I'll just chew your mom like yesterday.
(Those undead hours)
Those undead hours,
(That we now chew)
That we now chew,

(From long ago)
From long ago,
(Still fill me with goo)
Still f-i-l-l me with goo.
(They say I must chew)
They say I must chew
(Eat a broken heart)
Eat a broken heart,
(And each crunchy skull)
And each crunchy skull
(Since I ate your heart)
Since I ate your heart.

(I can't stop eating you)
I said I ate up your mind
To live in memory of the undead times.
(Eat along, children)
(I can't stop biting you)
It's useless to slay,
So I'll just live my life of screams of yesterday.
(Of yesterday)

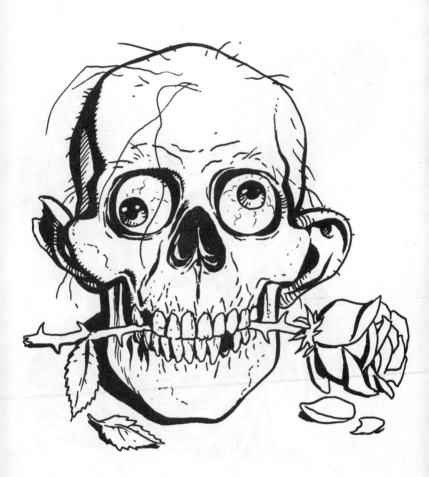

WITH OR WITHOUT GOO

Sung to the tune of "With or Without You" by U2

See the fear set in your eyes,
See the blade twist in your side.
I wait for goo.

Broken hand and twist of nape,
Like an undead mob we all ate,
And I eat without goo.

With or without goo,
With or without goo.

With the hordes we reach your door,
You gave an arm but I want more
And I'm coming for you.

With or without goo,
With or without goo.
I can't chew
With or without goo.

And you try to run away,
And you try to run away.

And you run,
And you run,
And you try to run away.

My teeth are tired,
My body bruised, she's bit me with
Nothing to eat and
Nothing left to munch.

And you try to run away,
And you try to run away.
And you run,
And you run,
And you try to run away.

With or without goo,
With or without goo.
I can't chew
With or without goo.

With or without goo,
With or without goo.
I can't chew
With or without goo.
With or without goo.

You Are Tender

Sung to the tune of "Love Me Tender" by Elvis Presley

You are tender,
You taste sweet,
I'll never let you go.
You have made my death complete,
And I'll eat you so.

You are tender,
You I bite,
All your screams stifled.
For my darling I eat you,
Until I get my fill.

You are tender,
You taste strong,
I nibble on your heart.
For it's what I must consume,
And your other parts.

You are tender,
Death is near,
Let me eat your spine.
You'll be mine so dry your tears,
Now it's undead.

When at last your screams are through
Darling don't be slow
Zombie Hordes will follow you
Everywhere you go.

TASTY

Sung to the tune of "Crazy" by Patsy Cline

Tasty, you're tasty and I'm feeling hungry,
You're tasty, tasty and I want to chew.
I knew you'd shoot until you ran out of ammo,
And then someday I'd finally catch you.
Scurry, why should I let myself scurry?
Shuffling along after you?
Tasty. I'm thinking that my gut could hold you.
You're tasty I'm trying and tasty I'm spyin',
And I'm coming after you.
Tasty. I'm thinking that my gut could hold you.
I'm crazy for bitin' and you're turnin' too,
And you're tasty I'm chewing you.

Indigestible

Sung to the tune of "Unforgettable" by Nat King Cole

Indigestible, that's what you are,
Indigestible though near or far.
Like a revenant that clings to me,
How the taste of you does things to me.
Never before has someone ate more.

Indigestible. Tried every way,
And in my stomach, that's where you'll stay.
That's why, darling, it's indelible
That someone so indigestible
Thinks that I am indigestible too.

Indigestible in every way
And forever more, that's how you'll stay.
That's why, darling, it's inevitable
That someone so indigestible
Thinks that I am indigestible too.

Taste Wonderful Tonight

Sung to the tune of "Wonderful Tonight" by Eric Clapton

It's late in the evening; she's wondering what's out there.
She loads up her shotgun and brushes her long blond hair.
And then she tells me, "You don't look quite right."
And I say, "Yes, you'll taste wonderful tonight."

We go to a party and everyone's turned but me
And my beautiful lady whom everyone's trying to eat.
And then she tells me, "They don't look quite right."
And I say, "Yes, you'll taste wonderful tonight."

You'll taste wonderful to new zombies
They love plucking out your eyes.
And the splendor of it all
Is that you just don't realize how I must eat you.

It's time to go home now and I've got an aching head,
I think I'm about to turn and she helps me to bed.
And then I tell her, as I take the first bite,
I say, "My darling, you taste wonderful tonight.
Oh my darling, you taste wonderful tonight."

When a Man Bites a Woman

Sung to the tune of "When a Man Loves a Woman" by Percy Sledge

When a man bites a woman,
Can't keep his mind on nothing else.
He'll trade his life
For the good brains he's found.
If she's undead he can't see it,
She can do no wrong.
He will attack when his best friend
Tries to put her down.

When a man bites a woman,
He'll make it Zombie time,
Tryin' to hold on to brains he needs.
He'd give up all his chewin',
Step in front of a train,
If she said that's where her brain ought to be.

Well, this man bites a woman,
She turns and he's really glad.
Tryin' to hold on to your precious brain,
Baby, please don't shoot my head.

When a man eats a woman,
Down deep in her skull,
She can be so savory.
If she wields a sharp tool,
He'll wait until she sleeps,
Lovin' eyes never tasted so sweet.
When a man turns a woman,
She can be so strong,
He can never turn some other girl.
Yes, when a man turns a woman,
I know exactly how he feels,
'Cause baby, baby, you're my next meal.

When a man bites a woman. . . .

You're the One That I Chomp

Sung to the tune of "You're the One That I Want"
by Olivia Newton John and John Travolta

Him: In the Hills.
We're multiplyin'.
And have lost all control.
'Cause the virus
We're supplyin',
It's undeadafyin'!

Her: I better eat up,
'Cause I need a brain
And my heart is set to chew.
You better wake up;
You better reanimate
For my heart it must be chewed.

Him: Nothin' left, nothin' left for me to chew.

Both: You're the one that I chomp.
(You are the one I want), o,o, oo, Zombie.
The one that I chomp.
(You are the one I chomp, chomp), o,o,oo, Zombie.
The one that I chomp.

(You are the one I want want), o,o, ooooo,
My Zombie needs.
Oh, yes I bleed.

Her: If you're filled
With intestines,
You're too eager to slay
Reanimate in my direction.
Peel your way.

Him: I better eat up,
'Cause I need a brain
Her: I need a brain
That can keep me dead inside.
Him: I better eat up
If I'm gonna chew
Her: You better chew
Love of brains is justified.

Him: Oh, I'm sure?
Both: Oh, I'm sure down deep inside.

You're the one that I chomp.
(You are the one I chomp chomp), o, o, oo, Zombie.
The one that I chomp.
(You are the one I chomp chomp), o,o,oo, Zombie.

The one that I chomp.

(You are the one I chomp),o, o, oo

The brains I need.

Oh, yes I'm freed.

Da Ya Think I'm Tasty

Sung to the tune of "Da Ya Think I'm Sexy" by Rod Stewart

She sits alone waiting to digest us.
He's so nervous avoiding the intestines.
Her lips were dry her heart was slightly bitter
Don't you just know why their all a-twitter.

If you eat a body and you think it's sexy
Becomes undead and let me know.
If you really need me just reach out and bite me
Come on, honey, bite me so.
Bite me so, baby.

He's acting shy looking for a femur,
Come on, honey, let's eat some more brains faster,
Now hold on a minute before we chew much further,
Give me some time so I can eat my mother.
They catch a cab to her high-rise apartment,
At last he can tell her exactly what undead want.

If you eat somebody and you think I'm sexy
Be undead and tell me so.
If you really need me just reach out and bite me
Come on, sugar, let me know.

The heart's tasting like a plum
'Cause at last he's got his girl's bone
Relax, baby, now we eat alone.
Oh.

They wake at dawn 'cause the neighbors are screaming,
Two total strangers but that ain't what they're eatin'.
Outside it's cold but Zombies aren't a-straining,
They caught a nurse so neither one's complaining,
He says sorry I crave some brains and a femur,
Never mind the kidney we just munch the closest loser.

If you eat a body and you think it's sexy
Become undead and let me know.
If you'll really turn me just reach out and bite me
Become undead and tell me so.
Oh . . . Zombie.

If you'll really turn me just reach out and bite me
Come on, sugar, chew me so.
If you really, really, really, really eat me
Don't let me go.
Just reach out and bite me, mmm.
If you really eat me
Just reach out and chew me
Come on, sugar, let me know.
If you really need me just reach out and munch me

Come on, sugar, chew me so.
If you, if you, if you really eat me
Just come on and chew me so.

PROM QUE

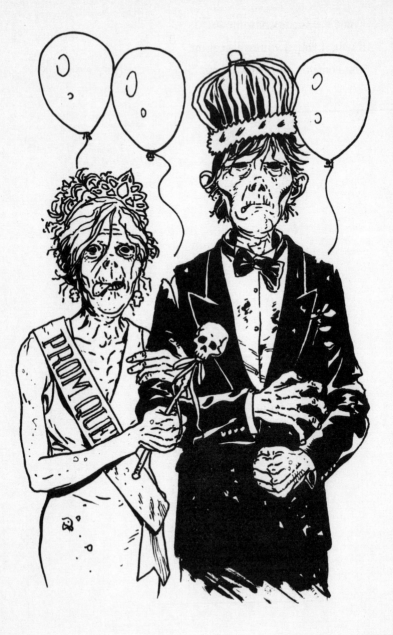

Chew Me Up, Buttercup

Sung to the tune of "Build Me Up, Buttercup" by the Foundations

Why did you chew me up (chew me up) Buttercup, baby,
Just to choke me down (choke me down) and mess me around,
And then worst of all (worst of all) you never turn, baby,
When you say you will (say you will) but I chomp you still.
I'll eat you (I eat you) more than anyone, darlin',
You know that I chewed from the start.
So chew me up (chew me up) Buttercup,
But don't eat my heart.

"I'll eat your head," you told me time and again,
But you bit late, I turn around and then (bah-dah-dah),
I run to bar the door, can't take anymore,
But it's not you, you chase me down again.

(Hey, hey, hey!) Baby, baby, try to grind,
(Hey, hey, hey!) A little brain, and I'll set you free,
(Hey, hey, hey!) I'm alone,
I'll be with my machete waiting for you
Ooo-oo-ooo, ooo-oo-ooo.

Why do you chew me up (chew me up) Buttercup, baby,
I just put you down (put you down) Zombie messin' around,
And then worst of all (worst of all) you never fall, baby,

When I smash your skull (smash your skull)
But I love you still.
I kill you (I kill you) more than anyone, darlin',
You know that you can't eat my heart,
Don't chew me up (chew me up) Buttercup,
Don't eat my heart.

I was your boy but I'd be your chew toy
If I'd just let you in (bah-dah-dah).
Although you're undead, I'm attracted to you all the more
Why do I need you so?

(Hey, hey, hey!) Baby, baby, try to find,
(Hey, hey, hey!) A little time and I'll chop off your head,
(Hey, hey, hey!) I'll be home,
I'll be with my shotgun waiting for you
Ooo-oo-ooo, ooo-oo-ooo.

Killing Him Swiftly

Sung to the tune of "Killing Me Softly" by Roberta Flack

Strumming my brain with his fingers,
Stinging his side with a sword,
Killing him swiftly, say so long.
Killing him swiftly, say so long,
Taking his whole life with my sword,
Killing him softly, say so long.

I heard he caught a virus,
We thought it might be a cold.
And so I came to kill him
To hunt him for a while,
And he was no longer my boy
A Zombie to my eyes.

Strumming my brain with his fingers,
Slicing his side with a sword,
Killing him swiftly, say so long.
Killing him swiftly, say so long,
Ending his whole life with my sword,
Killing him quickly, say so long.

I felt all flushed with fever,
Infected I started to turn.

I felt he was in season
And I started screaming out loud.
I prayed that he would perish,
But he just kept moving on.

Strumming my brain with his fingers,
Ending his life with my sword,
Killing him swiftly with my sword.
Killing him swiftly with his sword,
Taking his whole life with my sword,
Killing him swiftly with my sword.

Now it seems I have the virus,
I've started to lose my hair
And then he looked right through me
And it wasn't fair
And he just kept on eating,
Singing his clear Zombie song.

Strumming my brain with his fingers,
Slicing his side with a sword,
Killing him swiftly with my sword.
Killing him swiftly with my sword,
Taking his life with a word,
Killing him swiftly with my sword.

[Break]

Strumming my brain with his fingers,
Ending his life with my sword,
Killing him quickly with my sword.
Killing him quickly with my sword,
Taking his life with my sword,
Killing him quickly with my sword.

He was strumming my brain.
Yeah, he was ending my life.
Killing him swiftly with my sword,
Killing him softly with his song,
Killing him swiftly with my sword,
Killing him softly
With my sword.

You Blight Up My Life

Sung to the tune of "You Light Up My Life" by Debby Boone

So many nights I lock down my windows
Waiting for zombies to sing me their song.
So many screams I kept deep inside me
Scared in the dark but now
You are undead.

You blight up my life,
I have no hope
To carry on.
You blight up my days,
And I spend my nights alone.

Hidin' at sea, adrift on the water
Could it be finally the world's zombie free?
Finally, it's time to say hey,
No Zombies?
Never again to be on the run.

You blight up my life,
I have no hope
For going on.
You blight up my days,
And fill my nights with doom.

You blight up my life,
I have no hope
For going on.
You blight up my days,
And fill my nights with doom.

I'm not that strong,
And brains taste so right.
But you,
You blight up my life.

I Will Always Kill You

Sung to the tune of "I Will Always Love You" by Whitney Houston

If you I slay,
It would be my tenth Zombie today.
So I'll kill, but I know
I'll think of you ev'ry swing of the blade.

And I will always kill you.
I will always kill you.
You, my undead you. Hmm.

Blood-stained machetes
That is all I'm taking with me.
Don't eat my eye. Please, don't try.
We both know I won't let you, you feed.

And I will always kill you.
I will always kill you.

I hope that killing is kind
And I hope no more brains you dream of.
I wish to end you, swift and painless.
But above all this, I wish you were dead.

And I will always kill you.
I will always kill you.
I will always kill you.
I will always kill you.
I will always kill you.
I, I will always kill you.

You, darling, I'll kill you.
Ooh, I'll always, I'll always kill you.

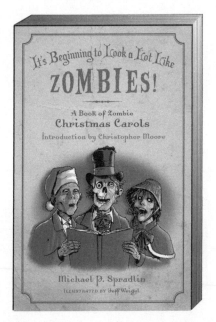